MONS DINER

by Danny Pearson
Illustrated by Seb Camagajevac

Titles in Ignite

Alien Sports TV	Jonny Zucker
Monster Diner	Danny Pearson
Team Games	Melanie Joyce
Mutant Baby Werewolf	Richard Taylor
Rocket Dog	Lynda Gore
The Old Lift	Alison Hawes
Spiders from Space	Stan Cullimore
Gone Viral	Mike Gould
The Ghost Train	Roger Hurn
Dog Diaries	Clare Lawrence

Badger Publishing Limited
Suite G08, Stevenage,
Hertfordshire SG1 2DX
Telephone: 01438 791037   Fax: 01438 791036
www.badgerlearning.co.uk

Monster Diner ISBN 978-1-84926-953-7

Publisher: Susan Ross
Senior Editor: Danny Pearson
Designer: Fiona Grant
Illustrator: Seb Camagajevac

MONSTER DINER

Contents

Chapter 1	**Kitchen hand wanted**	5
Chapter 2	**The kitchen**	q
Chapter 3	**The menu**	12
Chapter 4	**Panic in the diner**	18
Chapter 5	**V.I.P.**	23
Strange foods		30
Questions		32

Vocabulary:

urgent	kitchen
grunted	customers
interested	critic

Main characters:

David

Mr Wu

Chef

CHAPTER 1

Kitchen hand wanted

It was the summer holidays and David needed money.

He could not find a summer job anywhere.

That was, until he came across a sign in the window of a diner.

The sign read:

'Urgent – kitchen hand wanted for busy kitchen, apply round back.'

David could not see into the diner as it had blacked-out windows, and it looked as if you needed a pass to get through the front door.

He walked around the diner and knocked on the back door.

A small, strange-looking man opened up. "What do you want?" he asked.

The man looked out of breath and rushed off his feet.

"I am interested in the job in your front window," David told him.

Pots and pans could be heard crashing and falling on the floor from inside the kitchen.

With a sigh the man said, "I am Mr Wu. When can you start?"

"Right away!" David quickly answered.

"Good, come in and I will show you around, young man."

CHAPTER 2

The kitchen

"Here, you will need this," said Mr Wu, as he handed David an apron. "I hope you don't mind washing up, as there will be lots of pots, pans and plates to clean."

"No, I don't mind at all," replied David.

"Good, good," Mr Wu said, with a smile. "There are two rules you must follow if you are to work here. Number one, no talking to the Chef, he doesn't like talking."

David looked over at the Chef.

He was a huge man dressed in chefs'
clothes, topped off with a large chef's
hat. The Chef looked over and grunted.

He was a very odd-looking man and
David did not want to be in his bad
books.

"OK," said David. "And rule number
two?"

The small man looked David right in
the eyes and said, "You must never
leave the kitchen. You are not allowed
to go into the diner where our
customers eat."

CHAPTER 3

The menu

David had been working in the kitchen for over a week, now. The work was hard, but he did not mind.

He loved watching all of the strange foods that were being made by the Chef.

He had spotted dishes, such as beans on fish, sweet corn and ice cream, and tea served with a side order of squid.

Mr Wu would constantly run in and out of the kitchen, making sure everything was OK.

David could never manage to sneak a peek into the diner. There was a set of double doors that never seemed to be open at the same time.

The Chef would make the food and serve it through a hatch in the wall.

"Mr Wu, may I ask where you came up with such an interesting menu?" asked David.

Mr Wu stood still. "Why do you ask?"

"I was just wondering who would order tea with a side order of squid?" David said quietly.

"Why, don't you like my food?" snapped Mr Wu.

"No, no, I am sure it is lovely, it just all seems a little strange." David whispered.

Mr Wu stood up as tall as he could and said, "Well, if you have never tried any of the food, then don't question it. My customers seem to like my menu, so there."

Then he walked off into the diner.

David was surrounded by pots, pans and plates that needed to be cleaned.

He was just about to make a start on them, when he heard screams coming from the diner.

Mr Wu shouted through to the kitchen, "Chef, we need you in the diner now!"

The Chef ran towards the diner doors, but slipped on a fish head.

"Argh!" the Chef shouted as he fell to the floor with a crash.

David could not believe his eyes.
The Chef's hat had fallen off and now
David could see that a tiny creature was
sitting inside his head.

"Oops," the creature said, as it looked
up at David.

"Chef, help!" Mr Wu shouted.

David had to do something, so he broke
rule number two… he ran into the diner.

Chapter 4

Panic in the diner

The diner was full of more strange-looking creatures of all shapes and sizes. David stood still, as he could see all eyes were on him.

On a coat stand in the corner, he could see different human disguises hung up.

In the middle of the diner, a large creature looked like he was choking.

Mr Wu was trying to pat him on the back, but it wasn't helping.

Without thinking, David took a long run-up and aimed for the creature's stomach.

"Burpppppp!" went the creature, as a large steak, covered in dog hair with chocolate sauce, flew across the room.

Everyone stood there quietly for a second, then cheered.

"What is going on?" asked David.

Mr Wu bounced over to him and said, "Thank you, David, for helping. I know this may be a shock to you, but my diner serves monsters. Hey, we all have to eat somewhere, right?"

David nodded.

"So now you know, hopefully you will be able to keep this to yourself? I would love it if you could carry on working here?"

"Yes, of course," David said, while still in shock.

Another loud cheer came from the customers.

CHAPTER 5

V.I.P.

Work was great now that Chef and David were talking. He had even been asked by Chef to help him out with a rat problem the kitchen was having.

"David... Chef... we have a very important person coming to the diner today. He reviews food for the Monster Times newspaper," Mr Wu said. "We must make sure that everything is perfect."

David helped Chef to prepare the best squid and soil meal they could.

"Perfect!" said Chef with a grin.

"Not bad at all," Mr Wu said with a smile.

David looked on with a raised eyebrow, "Yes, urm… yummy!"

The food critic, Slugsworth, was sitting at his table. "I'm ready for my food, now!" he roared.

"Yes, right away sir," replied Mr Wu.

Chef didn't see that a rat had jumped under the plate cover as he was serving the meal through the hatch.

Mr Wu walked up to Slugsworth with the tray in his hand.

He set the plate down in front of him and lifted the lid. "Your meal, Sir," said Mr Wu.

"Oh no!" David and Chef said as they peered through the hatch.

Mr Wu was lost for words as he looked at the rat peeping out of the squid.

"What is this!?" shouted Slugsworth.

Mr Wu looked ill. "Sir, I am so sorry, I…"

"Squid, soil… and rat… my favourite!" Slugsworth shouted.

David, Chef and Mr Wu watched on with smiles on their faces as Slugsworth ate the lot.

Strange foods

There are many foods in the world that you may think are strange, but here are some that people in different countries eat every day.

Insects

Insects are eaten in many parts of the world. The only places that really don't eat insects are Europe and North America. The most popular insects are fried grasshoppers, crickets, scorpions, spiders and worms. Insects are high in protein and full of vitamins.

Fugu

Fugu is the Japanese word for the poisonous puffer fish. It is filled with enough poison to be deadly. Only specially-trained chefs, who have passed an official test, can cut the fish.

A lot of people have died while eating this very deadly dish.

Haggis

Haggis is a Scottish dish, made with the minced heart, liver and lungs of a sheep, mixed with onion, spices, oatmeal, salt and stock, and boiled in the sheep's stomach for a few hours.

Haggis is available all year-round in Scottish supermarkets, and is made with a fake casing rather than a sheep's stomach.

Questions

What did the sign read in the window
of the diner?

What was the name of the owner of
the diner?

What were the two rules?

Name one of the dishes David saw in
the kitchen.

What is the name of the food critic?

What is the most disgusting food you
have ever eaten?